Rosemary Hayes

The Gremlin
Buster

Illustrated by
Kate Aldous

PUFFIN BOOKS

For Oliver

PUFFIN BOOKS

Published by the Penguin Group
Penguin Books Ltd, 27 Wrights Lane, London W8 5TZ, England
Viking Penguin, a division of Penguin Books USA Inc.
375 Hudson Street, New York, New York 10014, USA
Penguin Books Australia Ltd, Ringwood, Victoria, Australia
Penguin Books Canada Ltd, 2801 John Street, Markham, Ontario, Canada L3R 1B4
Penguin Books (NZ) Ltd, 182–190 Wairau Road, Auckland 10, New Zealand

Penguin Books Ltd, Registered Offices: Harmondsworth, Middlesex, England

First published by Viking 1990
Published in Puffin Books 1991
10 9 8 7 6 5 4 3 2 1

Text copyright © Rosemary Hayes, 1990
Illustrations copyright © Kate Aldous, 1990
All rights reserved

The moral right of the author and illustrator has been asserted

Printed in England by Clays Ltd, St Ives plc
Filmset in Times (Linotron 202)

PUFFIN BOOKS

THE GREMLIN BUSTER

What *do* you do when you find a gremlin inside your washing machine?

Peter doesn't know what a gremlin is. Then, one night, he's unlucky enough to meet the one that's been messing up the washing machine. But the washing machine is only the beginning. The gremlin is the nastiest and most mischievous creature Peter has ever come across and soon it's turning the whole house topsy turvy with Peter hot at its tail. But even if he can catch it, how can he get rid of it? It's Peter's Gran who eventually comes up with the unexpected answers.

After a career in advertising in New York and London, Rosemary Hayes went to live in Australia, where she took a writing course at Monash University. Since returning to live in Britain, she has written several information books for children. She now runs a small publishing house in rural Cambridgeshire where she lives with her husband, their three children and an assortment of animals.

Chapter One

SHUDDER, GRIND, BANG!
Everyone heard the noise.
   Peter,
   Peter's mum,
   Mr Jones the repair man
and all the people in the
street outside.

Shudder, grind, bang.
Shudder, grind, BANG!
Bang, bang, shudder,
GRIND!

Mr Jones stood and frowned.

Peter's mum stood beside him and glared.

Peter shifted from one foot to the other.

"It's a very *old* washing machine," said Mr Jones, at last.

Peter's mum sniffed: "There's plenty of good life left in that machine," she said. "If you ask me, it's careless repair work." She stared hard at Mr Jones.

Mr Jones said nothing.

"You've been to mend it three times," went on Peter's mum. "It works for a week and then

it breaks down."

Shudder, grind, BANG.

"There's a gremlin in that machine," said Mr Jones.

Peter looked up: "What's a gremlin?"

"A gremlin," said Peter's mum, "is something that gets into a machine and wrecks it.

People only talk about gremlins
when they don't know what's
wrong." She stared at Mr Jones
again, picked up her mug of tea
and went out of the room.

Mr Jones sighed. He put his
tool bag on the floor and knelt
down. He laid out his tools
and turned off the machine.

Shudder, shudder, grind, grind, stop.

Peter watched Mr Jones work.

Mr Jones undid some screws. He peered inside the washing machine, took out some parts and looked at them. He shook his head, put them back again, replaced the screws, wiped his hands and stood up. He turned the machine on again.

Purr, purr, whine, whine. It worked perfectly.

"What have you done?" asked Peter.

Mr Jones scratched his head.

"Nothing," he said. "That's the trouble. I can't find

anything wrong."

"But it's working now."

"And next week, it'll break
down again and your mum'll be
on the phone, yelling at me
again."

He sighed: "I tell you, son, there *is* a gremlin in that machine!"

"You mean a real something inside the machine, messing it all up?"

"Yes, a *gremlin*!"

"Are gremlins real, then?"

Mr Jones smiled and put his finger to his lips:

"Shh! It'll hear you."

Then he ruffled Peter's hair, picked up his tool bag and walked out of the door.

When Mr Jones had gone, Peter's mum sat down wearily and kicked off her shoes.

"It's not that old," she said. "And we can't afford a new one." She looked really worried.

Peter said nothing. But he was thinking hard.

Next time mum used the machine, he listened very carefully.

Purr, purr, whine, whine. Nothing wrong.

And the next time.

And the next time.

Nothing wrong.

But the next time he *thought*

he heard something just a bit different.

Purr, purr, whine–click, whine–click.

That night, Peter took a torch and a screwdriver up to his bedroom. He waited until mum, dad and his sister Kate were asleep. Then he went downstairs,

on tiptoe, not making a sound.
He opened the kitchen door
very, very slowly and went in.
He crept across the floor,
feeling his way in the dark,
until he came to the washing
machine. Quiet as a mouse, he
knelt down beside it and little
by little, undid the screws
that held the back panel in
place. Then, with one quick
move, he pulled the panel off
and shone his torch inside.

It was hard to know who
was most surprised.

Peter had such a shock that he

fell over backwards and dropped his torch.

But, inside the machine, the gremlin, caught red-handed (or green-handed because the gremlin was green), fell from the top to the bottom of the machine, where it became caught up on a screw.

Peter picked up his torch and scrambled on to his knees. For a moment he thought the gremlin had escaped. Then he saw it, dangling from the screw. It was hissing with rage.

For a few seconds, they stared at each other. The gremlin hissed and Peter's mouth hung

open in surprise. At last he
found his voice:

"What are you *doing*?" he
whispered.

"Untangle me, you stupid boy,"
hissed the gremlin, wriggling
and trying to free himself.

Peter shone his torch full in

the gremlin's face. It blinked
and spat. Then it wriggled
some more. Then it hissed, and
it called Peter all the rude
names it knew.

Peter waited. After what
seemed a very long time, the
gremlin stopped swearing and
spitting, hissing and wriggling.
It dangled silently on the
screw and a tear ran down its
cheek. Peter didn't know what
to do. What *do* you do when you
find a green gremlin inside your
washing machine? He almost felt
sorry for it.

He cleared his throat.

"If I unhook you, will you

tell me who you are and what you're doing?"

The gremlin nodded miserably.

Very carefully, Peter untangled it from the screw. If he hadn't had a tight grip, the gremlin would have wriggled free and disappeared. But Peter was prepared and he held on, even when the gremlin bit him.

Chapter Two

"Ouch! That hurt!" said Peter.
The hand that held the
gremlin was getting very
scratched and bitten. Peter had
the torch in his other hand and

he shone it round the kitchen. Where could he put this struggling, nasty green THING?

The gremlin kept on biting and kicking.

"Stop it!" whispered Peter. "Stop it or I'll squash you! I'll put you in the mixer . . . I'll bake you in the oven . . . I'll flush you down the loo!"

The gremlin bit and kicked even harder.

Peter flashed the beam of the torch round and round the kitchen. Then, at last, he saw the answer.

He put his torch between his teeth, picked up an oven glove

from beside the cooker, and pushed the gremlin right down inside. He held the top firmly closed.

Muffled screams came from inside:

"I'll get you for this, you stupid boy! Let me out!"

The oven glove became alive. It swung from side to side, then up and down and round and round, full of furious gremlin.

Peter couldn't hear everything it said. But what he did hear was extremely rude.

Holding the glove out in front of him, Peter went over to the light switch. He turned it on and searched until he found an elastic band. He wound this tightly round the top of the oven glove, put the glove down on the kitchen table and went to the sink to wash his sore hand.

He kept his eye on the glove, though. The lump of gremlin inside still wriggled.

He was just drying his hands when there was a thud. The oven glove was on the floor. The gremlin had wriggled it right off the table.

Peter picked it up. The lump inside was very still.

No squirms. No wriggles.

"Are you all right?"

No answer.

Peter poked the lump.

Nothing.

He poked it again. Still nothing.

Peter was worried. He didn't want to hurt the gremlin. He just wanted to stop it messing up the washing machine.

"I hope I haven't killed it," he thought. "Perhaps it can't breathe in there."

Very carefully, he unwound the elastic band from the top of the glove. He was just peering inside, when . . .

WHEEEEEEEE!

Something shot past his ear. The glove was empty.

The gremlin had gone!

Peter looked everywhere.

He looked under the table, behind the cooker, inside the cupboards and even down the plug hole. He peered into the washing machine. But the gremlin had completely disappeared.

Then he heard a very nasty laugh. Not quite a chuckle – more of a cackle, followed by a hiss.

Peter swung round. The laugh came from behind him.

There it was again. Above him.

No, it wasn't – it was down on the floor.

Peter was spinning round, trying to see where the laugh came from, but he couldn't. It came from ten different places at once.

BRRRRRRR! Now there was a different noise, from the cooker. The automatic timer was on. Quickly Peter turned it off.

He didn't want the whole family coming downstairs.

BRRRRRRR! It started again – and this time Peter couldn't stop it.

Then he noticed that the cooker was heating up. It was getting hotter and hotter. Peter turned everything off, but it made no difference.

There was another noise. WHRRRRRRRRR!

The electric mixer was mixing, all on its own. It was going faster and faster and faster. So fast, that soon it would take off and fly across the room. Peter rushed over to it, but just as he reached it, the whirling blades slowed down and the machine was still.

Then the electric light went out.

Peter fumbled round and found his torch.

The automatic timer still rang and the cooker still glowed in the darkness. Peter stumbled towards it but before he reached it everything suddenly stopped.

Peter leant up against the sink. What next?

But there was silence. Except for a faint – and very nasty – laugh.

And he thought he heard
someone mutter:

"Stupid humans. I'll
show them!"

But he couldn't be sure.

Peter didn't wait for anything else to happen. He went out of the kitchen and climbed the stairs to bed.

Chapter Three

The next day was Saturday. Peter was so tired he thought he'd stay in bed for a bit. Suddenly he heard screams coming from downstairs. He jumped out of bed and rushed down to the kitchen.

"Aahhhhh . . .!"

Mum was in the middle of the room; her hands were over her ears and her hair stood on end.

"Aahhhhh . . .!"

"Wow!" said Peter.

The cooker had gone mad. Breakfast was about to go into orbit. There were four eggs bouncing high into the air from their saucepan. The milk had boiled and now it ran over the cooker and down on to the floor in a brown, stinking goo.

"There's milk everywhere!" said Peter.

"I didn't put all that milk in the saucepan!" said mum. "Where's it all coming from?"

Peter slithered and slipped his way over to the stove.

"Pull out the electric plug," he said. Mum pulled it out.

Gradually, the eggs stopped bouncing, the saucepan stopped jumping and the milk stopped boiling over.

All the noise had woken Kate, Peter's sister. She came into the kitchen, rubbing her eyes.

She stared at the mess in the kitchen.

"YUK!" she said, and walked out.

Then dad rushed in, only half-shaved, wearing his vest and underpants.

"What's happening?"

Peter's mum was busy mopping up the mess.

"Something's gone wrong with the cooker," she said,

between mops. "I don't know
what's the matter with the
machines in this house. First
the washing machine, now the
cooker. What's next, I wonder?"

Peter's dad scratched his
soapy chin and frowned.

"I suppose we'd better get the
repair man in," he said.

Peter's mum squeezed out the floorcloth. "Huh! Repair men!" she muttered.

Peter said nothing about the gremlin. There was no point. No one in the family would believe him – except perhaps his Gran. Then he remembered. Of *course*, Gran was supposed to be coming to stay. Peter really liked his Gran. She was big and noisy and she had an answer for everything. She might even know what to do about a bad-tempered gremlin. But, best of all, she'd promised to bring him a very special birthday present this time. It was too special to post, she'd said, so he'd have to wait until she came to stay.

"When's Gran coming?" asked Peter.

"Today," said mum. Then she turned to dad:

"You'd better fix those shelves."

"Umm," said dad and went back upstairs.

They didn't have a cooked breakfast that morning. They ate cereal instead.

Everyone else had left the room, but Peter still felt hungry.

He decided to make some toast.
He took out two slices of bread
and put them in the toaster.

Then he stood looking out of
the window, waiting for the
toast to pop up.

WHAM!

Suddenly, a bullet-hard, burnt
piece of toast hurtled across
the room and hit him on the

nose. Peter just had time to say:

"OUCCHH!" when WHAM!

Another piece, just as hard and just as black, hit him even harder – this time on the ear.

Peter rushed over to the toaster.

"That hurt. You wait. I'll

get you, you little green vandal!"

He thought he saw a glimpse of green. And he certainly heard something – something that sounded like a cackling, hissing, spitting sort of laugh. Very nasty it was, too.

Peter rubbed his sore nose and his sore ear and went into the lounge to watch his favourite Saturday programme. He sat down and turned on the telly.

The screen was blank.

Peter twiddled the knobs. He switched off the set and then switched it on again. The screen was still blank.

Then something flashed across. But it was so fast, he couldn't read it.

It flashed again:

HUMANS ARE STUPID!

Peter sat bolt upright.

Surely the gremlin couldn't get

into the TELLY too! Another
flash:

GREMLINS ARE CLEVER
GREMLINS ARE BEST

Then there was a pause, and it
flashed again:

GREMLINS ARE HERE
TO STAY!

"Oh no, you're NOT,"
shouted Peter, turning off the
telly. "You wait till my Gran
gets here. She'll fix you!"

He looked at his watch. Then
he frowned. It couldn't be as
late as that. He looked at
the clock on the wall. It said
a different time. He got up and
went to look at the kitchen

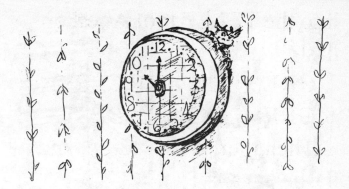

clock. That said something else.

The gremlin had been at all the clocks, too.

"Peter," shouted mum, from upstairs.

"Yes?"

"Gran's going to sleep in your room. You'll have to sleep in the lounge tonight. Come and move your things, there's a good boy."

Peter went into his room. Dad

had been putting up some
shelves and his drill was lying
on the floor. Peter walked
carefully round it.

Mum and dad were making up
the bed with clean sheets and an

electric blanket. Gran always liked an electric blanket.

Peter collected his things and went downstairs past Kate's room. Her walkman was over her head and she was humming along to a pop tune. As Peter went past her door, she suddenly stopped and frowned.

"Hey, Peter. Come here and listen. Something's gone wrong with this tape. It sounds like someone's laughing in the middle of the song."

Peter put his things down on the stairs and went into Kate's room. She took off her headphones and handed them to him.

Rather nervously, Peter put them on and listened. The song was blaring out, loud and clear, but he could also hear another voice.

"Stupid humans!" it said, over and over again, in time to the music. Then there was a nasty, hissing, cackling laugh.

Slowly, Peter took off the headphones and put them down on a chair.

"Sounds a bit funny," he said. "You'd better take it back to the shop."

Chapter Four

Peter wandered about the house. He was missing all the Saturday telly programmes. He went to find his dad.

"Dad. Can you fix the telly?"

"Not now, Peter, I'm busy," said dad. He was drilling holes in Peter's bedroom wall for the last shelf.

Peter went to find mum.

"Mum. Can you fix the telly?"

Mum was back in the kitchen.

She was looking suspiciously at the cooker. She had turned it on again and it *seemed* to be working perfectly.

"Never mind the telly," she said. "It's nearly lunch time. You can set the table for me."

Peter sighed and got some knives and forks out of a

drawer. He walked past the cooker, keeping as far away from it as possible, but it looked quite normal. "The gremlin," thought Peter, "must be busy somewhere else."

They all sat down to lunch. The meal was fine; the cooker had worked perfectly. The house was peaceful.

"Kate," said mum, after lunch, "could you go and hoover upstairs, please? Gran's coming later and I'd like to have the house looking clean."

Grumbling, Kate mounted the

stairs, the hoover clumping
behind her. Soon, a familiar
sound filled the house.

Vrrrruuuum, vrrrruuuum.

Mum made a cake and put it in
the oven to bake.

Still the hoover droned on.

Vrrrruuuum, vrrrruuuum.

Then, suddenly, there was another noise, even louder than the hoover.

"AHHHHHHHH! AAAAAAAHHHHHHHHH! HELLLLLLLLP!"

Mum, dad and Peter all raced upstairs.

Mum got to the top of the stairs first. She stopped dead and her hands flew to her mouth. Dad and Peter crashed to a halt behind her.

Kate's head was almost touching the ceiling. The hoover had gone mad. The carpet on the landing had been torn

away and had lifted right up.
It was like a huge waving sea
being sucked by a throbbing
monster. Kate was hanging on,
being tossed about like a ship
in a storm.

"Wow!" said Peter.

"AHHHHHHHH!" screamed
Kate, bouncing up and down,

and then, "OUCCHH!" as her head banged on the ceiling.

Mum dived underneath the waves of carpet and found the plug. She pulled it from the socket in the wall.

THUD! Kate and the hoover landed on the ground.

While dad and mum were comforting Kate and trying to straighten the carpet, Peter went and looked in his room.

First he noticed the shelves. Dad's new shelves. Before lunch, they had been straight. Now they leant drunkenly down the wall. Mum had put some books on the shelves for Gran and now

these lay in a heap on the
floor. Peter bent down to pick
them up, but then he noticed
something else. The bed was
moving!

He went over and pulled back
the covers. The electric
blanket was heaving up and down.
Peter was about to yell for mum

when he heard *another* scream –
coming from downstairs. He
rushed to the door and, as he
went out, he *thought* he saw a
small green something, and he
certainly heard a nasty laugh.
But he didn't stop. He ran
downstairs.

Kate's bumps and bruises
were forgotten. Now she and
mum and dad all stood by the
kitchen door, gawping.

"My *cake*!" yelled mum.

"Wow!" said Peter.

"I'll go and get a spade,"
said dad.

"And some wellies!" said
mum.

"It's coming to get us!" said Kate.

Mum's cake had risen and risen and risen. It had burst right out of the oven, and was filling up the whole of the kitchen. It was coming at them faster and faster.

"Quick," said mum. "Shut the door."

Kate, Peter and mum all leant against the door and just managed to get it shut.

"Phew!" said Kate. "At least it's only in the kitchen."

"No, it's not. Look!" Peter pointed at the bottom of the door. Goo was seeping underneath. More and more was coming at them. They backed down the passage.

BANG! The front door slammed.

"WHAT IS GOING ON IN THIS HOUSE?" roared a voice.

Gran had arrived.

"What's the matter with you all? Why wasn't there anyone to meet me at the bus . . ."

At that moment, dad rushed in, wearing wellies and holding a spade.

"You're early, Gran," he panted. Then he opened the kitchen door and started to dig.

"No, I'm not," said Gran, her eyes widening.

Peter looked at his watch. He'd forgotten all the clocks were wrong.

Gran looked inside the kitchen and turned to Peter and Kate:

"Go and get some buckets and

more shovels or spades –
anything. Hurry! And wellies
for everyone."

Peter and Kate rushed off and
came staggering back with
wellies, buckets, spades and
lots of other useful things

from the garden shed.

Gran hitched up her skirt and put on the nearest wellies.

"Come on, you lot," she said, attacking the goo with a shovel. "Let's get this mess cleared up."

Chapter Five

It took a long time to clear up the mess. When at last it was done, Gran made a pot of tea. Peter hovered near by.

"Have you got my birthday present, Gran?"

But Gran didn't answer. She just smiled. Then she sat down at the kitchen table and sipped her tea.

"Gran. Have you . . ." Peter began.

"Yes love, I have got your
present. But never mind *that*. I
want to know what's going on
in this house. Your mum says
it's a fault in the wiring. I
don't believe a word of it."

Peter shook his head:

"It's not the wiring," he said.

"What is it then?"

Peter took a deep breath:

"It's a *gremlin*," he
whispered.

Gran banged her fist on the
table so that her cup rattled in
its saucer.

"HA! I thought as much. A
gremlin, eh?" Then she started
to chuckle.

"Do you know about gremlins, Gran?" asked Peter.

"Know about gremlins? I should think I do! Nasty, bad-tempered things."

"Can you get rid of them?"

"Well," said Gran, taking another sip of tea. "As a matter of fact, I think I can. I happen to have just the thing to fix your gremlin."

"What's that?"

Gran smiled. "That," she said,
"is a secret." Then she
chuckled. "A birthday secret."

"Oh, please tell me, Gran!"
But Gran shook her head:
"You wait and see, my love."

Gran was very tired. She'd had a long journey and she'd worked hard helping to clear up the house. She decided to go to bed early. Peter went up to say goodnight.

Gran was tucked into bed. On the table beside her was her teasmade. It was plugged in, ready for her morning cup of tea. Peter looked worried and pointed at it:

"Gran, don't you think the . . ."

"Shh!" said Gran. "Don't you worry about me, Peter. I know what I'm doing."

As Peter went out of the

room, he noticed a box beside the bed. As he looked at it, the box seemed to move.

He was about to say something, but Gran shooed him out.

It was the middle of the night and suddenly, everyone was awake.

The telly was on.

The hoover was hoovering.

The cooker's timer was ringing.

Dad's drill whirred.

And Kate's walkman played Scottish reels.

Peter stumbled out of his bed
in the lounge and went to see
his Gran.

She was sitting up in bed,
laughing and laughing. Her
teasmade alarm was ringing and,
from the teasmade to the window,
Peter saw a trail of small, wet
footprints. He ran to the
window, and was just in time to

watch the wet, green gremlin climbing down the drainpipe. He could hear it swearing and hissing and spitting. When it reached the ground it ran away across the garden without a backward glance.

Peter turned to look at Gran – and saw, curled up on her chest, a very small, very

fluffy, black kitten.

Gran was laughing so much
that tears ran down her cheeks.
She wiped her eyes and held out
the kitten to Peter:

"Happy birthday," she said,
still chuckling.

Peter held the little bundle
of fur and stroked it gently.
The kitten looked up at him

and yawned.

"Is it really for me, Gran?"

"Of course it is, my love. I know you've always wanted one."

Peter sat down on the edge of the bed and went on stroking the kitten. Soon it closed its eyes and started to purr like a motorbike.

Peter grinned: "Thanks, Gran."
He was so busy looking at his
kitten that it was a minute or
two before he realized that all
the noises had stopped. The
house was quiet again. No
hoover, no drill, no telly, no
walkman. Even the teasmade was
quiet. There was complete
silence. He looked up at his
Gran.

"Everything's stopped!"
Gran looked very pleased
with herself.

"You've fixed it, haven't you,
Gran? You've fixed the gremlin!"
Gran nodded and grinned
broadly. Peter's eyes were wide.

"How did you do it?"

Gran pointed to the kitten:

"With that," she said.

"What! Was the gremlin scared of the *kitten*?" asked Peter.

Gran nodded, beginning to chuckle again:

"Terrified! It turned bright yellow! Gremlins can't stand being anywhere near a black cat. It's the one thing that frightens them."

"Has it gone for good, then?"

Gran nodded: "As long as you have a black cat in the house, you'll never have another gremlin."

Peter looked down at the

purring black bundle. Lazily,
it half opened one eye.

"You'd better stay here for a
good long time then, kitten,"
he said. Then he turned to
Gran. "Do you know what I'm
going to call it?"

"I can guess," said Gran.

"GREMLIN!" they both
shouted together.